Confessions

A collection Of Prose And Poetry

Benj Gabun Sumabat

Ukiyoto Publishing

All global publishing rights are held by

Ukiyoto Publishing

Published in 2022

Content Copyright © Benj Gabun Sumabat

ISBN 9789360160999

All rights reserved.
No part of this publication may be reproduced, transmitted, or stored in a retrieval system, in any form by any means, electronic, mechanical, photocopying, recording or otherwise, without the prior permission of the publisher.

The moral rights of the author have been asserted.

This is a work of fiction. Names, characters, businesses, places, events, locales, and incidents are either the products of the author's imagination or used in a fictitious manner. Any resemblance to actual persons, living or dead, or actual events is purely coincidental.

This book is sold subject to the condition that it shall not by way of trade or otherwise, be lent, resold, hired out or otherwise circulated, without the publisher's prior consent, in any form of binding or cover other than that in which it is published.

I dedicate this book to all lost souls; I hope we will soon find our place in this world.

"Death must be so beautiful. To lie in the soft brown earth, with the grasses waving above one's head, and listen to silence. To have no yesterday, and no tomorrow. To forget time, to forgive life, to be at peace."

-Sylvia Plath, The Bell Jar

Contents

Confession	1
Hang Me Like A Painting	4
I Am A Poet	6
Faceless	8
Making Out With Poems	10
To My Mothers,	12
Roses Grew, Outside My Body	14
Runaway	15
If I Could Just Read You Like A Novel	17
No One	18
Up there	21
When I see you	22
Incense	24
City Lights	25
Something	27
You	28
Help Is Available, Speak With Someone Today	29
A Journey Is A Work Of Art	31
This Town	32
I Am Writing This Poem Inside A Bus	33
To Hurt Someone	35
It's The Warmth That A Pair Of Socks Give	36
The City I Don't Like…	38

Part Of Me	39
Emptiness	40
To Whom It May Concern	41
Solitude	43
As I Walk Along The Streets Of Diliman	44
Time To Grieve	45
How Can I?	46
I know that I will burn everything	47
Never will I	48
Happiness Is A Choice?	49
About the Author	*50*

Confession

Bless me father, for I have sinned
it has been…
three years since my last confession.
These, oh! This are—is my
sins—sin… Do I have a sin?
Yes, I do! I am sad and depressed
and sad and depressed…
and I am truly sorry for all my sins…
Are you sad and depressed Father?
Do I have to feel sorry for being depressed?
For being sad?
"I think you lack in Faith for the Jesus Christ our savior,
pray, and attend Sunday mass".
I tried to pray, Father.
If Jesus did not hear my shouting voice at night,
In pain
In desperation
In Agony

In what language he only understands our prayer?

I attend Sunday mass, Father!

I meditate the mysteries of the rosary;

I pray the novena for Mother of Perpetual Help!

In what language they only understand our prayer?

"You must accept the suffering my son,

for it will bear you fruit and place in heaven."

I want to be in heaven! with the cute little angels,

Golden gates, and garden of Eve!

Yes, Father, I shall accept my sufferings!

Give me more suffering, Oh God!

And let me bear more fruits and a larger place in heaven!

O my God, I am heartily sorry for having offended Thee,

and I detest all my sins because of thy just punishments,

but most of all because they offend Thee…

"May our Lord and God, Jesus Christ,

through the grace and mercies of his love for humankind,

forgive you all your transgressions.

And I, an unworthy priest, by his power given me,

*forgive and absolve you from all your sins,
in the name of the Father and of the Son
and of the Holy Spirit…"*

Amen.

"Give thanks to the Lord for He is good."

His mercy endures forever.

"Your sins are forgiven. Go in peace."

Thanks be to God.

Hang Me Like A Painting

Hang me like a painting
In famous museums,
In Louvre, Metropolitan, or Vatican—
No! not in Vatican, I'm no holy!
in Louvre! Yes! Beside Monalisa!
Or along The raft of the Medusa.

Hang me like a painting
Unmoved yet treasured,
I wonder what it feels; to do nothing,
Yet still be admired! Oh Heavenly beings,
Hang me!

Hang me like a painting
In a wide, populated, vast space
Watch my body float, eyes popping, skin turned grapes!
Admire me like art, people! Critic me! Praise me!

For eternity, hang me!
Suspended above the furious animal,
Which, mad with agony and fury,
Like a picture of demoniac rage.

Oh, hang me, I beg you!
Let me fly and be free;
Don't cry, don't, don't, don't…
I am an art, admire me!
Remember me for eternity!

Gaze upon the abysmal depths,
Of the sky; night a bright
I am there! Floating with the dusts, stars,
And with the moon which everybody admires!

I Am A Poet

I am a poet

I am a poet

I am a poet

I am a poet, and I shall not die

I shall never vanish

I am with words, rhymes, lines

I am tied with the universe, in every matter, in every dust

I am a poet, and I shall not die

I shall never wither

I am the sacred Lotus that shall thrive,

In every river, streams, and lakes…

I am a poet, and I shall not die

I am the manifestation of the universe

Vague, omnipotent, dark, and ferocious;

I am the enormous cloud of dust and gas that gave birth to stars—

I shall never perish nor disappear…

I am the air, water, land, and fire

I am with every atom and every cell,

I am rain, sun, sunset, and sunrise

I shall dawn with sunburst and ecstasy

Because I am a poet, and no one can stop me…

Faceless

A friend once asked me, "How does depression affects you?"

depression is an infinite abyss in you,

every step is a step on a slippery floor, covered with

layers of dark-green algae,

depression is waking up when the sky already

succumbed to darkness, and staying awake until—

the hot, burning, colossus, sun; scorches your fragile-cracked skin

depression is the end of summer—nostalgic

and regretful—wishing that you could have done more

than do nothing.

depression is drinking a new brand of coffee,

familiar but alienating.

depression is crucifixion, both hands and feet—nailed

deep onto the edge of your bed; as you struggle to move, move, move while the Roman soldiers of anxiety and psychosis whips you

endlessly—like a rushing stream, flowing, rushing, flowing…

depression is inescapable, like your own shadow—

it may not be there but it's there…

and when the sky retreats for respite,

your endless agony commences…

Making Out With Poems

And it's dark again—

he opened the creaking door, naked and solemn.

he grabbed my waist, closer, tighter, closer…

he tucked it in, sweaty, hard, painful—like run on sentences

confusing, indirect, and nimble…

his veiny hands: firm and fragile vines that thrives in wilderness

caresses me with words, metaphors, and everything beautiful.

his lips were the taste of bourbon whiskey—soft, sweet, and rough

like an acid scorching and devouring my earthly brown skin,

I'm out of breath, *I moan, I moan, I moan*

I moan with delight, hunger, desperation, passion, and pleasure

like tentacles spiraling out from my stomach,

crawling through my esophagus, I screamed! My eyes turned canvas…

he is the cupid who struck an arrow in every pore of my skin—

a whirlwind developing in my abdomen,

I was knocked off my feet and beg him to stay, stay, stay

Stay so I could write rhymes and images and words

on my paper…

He just turned, laughed—and promised,

That he'll come again, another day…

To My Mothers

Your hands are the moon in the sky
held open, to carry me out of my darkness
to shine rays of hope in every corner of my heart
to give me warmth in a cold and lonely night

Your face is the sun in the sky
reminding me that even after a storm
a new day shall dawn—a new chance shall be gained
the homeliest face that holds the purest and
strongest love one can ever possess…

Your voice is the music in the heart
Even the finest composers can't produce
A soothing, simple, and dreamy tone you have
And even the finest artisans can't create an
Instrument of comfort like you have…

my words
my rhymes
my music
my art
my poem
will never capture your love, care, and sacrifices

No stars can even outshine your light
no moon, no sun, no music, no art—
could ever replace the love you give and continue to give

To my mothers, I am who I am because of you…

Roses Grew, Outside My Body

Rainy nights can be a bed of Roses,
can be a bed of thorns,
raindrops can be voices,
can be little dreams waiting to be born…

>Voices imprisoned in my temple…
>some days, they're calm,
>but mostly, they're in chaos,
>do you know how it feels to be imprisoned?
>In your own self?

They tried to escape and cut their way out;
but rivers of red Roses flowed, it dripped to the white old tiles—
it smelled like rusting iron, it feels thick and velvety
they seemed to find their way out,

Roses grew, outside my body…

Runaway

I'll soon leave the society—like a fleeting raven—
in the dark nights—black as the thick ink;
I'll run straight to the woods, to the sea, to the—
desert...
I'll abandon the screeching pain—shivering spines
heart embraced by scorching barbwires
I'll withdraw what the society shoved and tubed
down through my throat
even the pain of a rumbling stomach—tangled
intestines,
I'll vomit every thing—every bits
I'll soon leave this society—
but the world and every generation that shall come—
will be reminded...
That I once lived and tried to live...

If I could write everything I feel, it will be filled with scribbles

Do poets really feel something?

No…

Poets feel everything

If I Could Just Read You Like A Novel

If I could just read you like a novel—
I will roll every syllable on my tongue,
I will cherish every scene,
I will reread every chapter—
whatever it may be…

I will read you forever, so
please do not turn the page,
please do not let the clock run,
I shall always be here,

at the chapter where you left me…

No One

No one heard

no one saw

no one cared

no one came

I know it's getting bad again,

when the skies

turn darker

when flowers

starts to wither

when all I feel

is void and nothing and void and nothing

No one noticed

no one believed

no one helped

no one tried

I cried a river; yet the river ain't enough—

shouted until my voice cracked and I spit blood

I was drowning,
still, I grasped
I tried to
write, yet no words
 I tried to live,
yet no life…

Left untouched; touched

The pen dropped
the ink spilled
the paper was left—
left untouched

The writer once dreamed,
of becoming one—
one with his soul,
with his heart and mind

He picked the pen
cleaned the ink
fixed the paper—
he started writing

a new dawn awaits…

Up there

I'm always been an admirer of the stars, sun, sky, celestial beings, and even the flying birds. To see the beauty up there while grounded and chained with the chaos down here. On how the stars twinkle in a dusty, pitch-black night sky. On how the moon feels so whole even though there are phases it's broken and incomplete. Sometimes, I ask myself *"Why do you like things up there?"* Yes, I love and adore things that are seen, heard, felt, and experienced—but always out of my reach. I relish hanged paintings, actually, I covet them. I envy things up there. Like paintings, someday I'll pose with a string attached to a wall—to float in silence within the vastness of the cosmos. *To join the stars, sun, sky, celestial beings, and even the flying birds.*

When I see you

Our path crossed,
Like a grain of dust
Floating on the air, under the ray—
Of sunlight.
The universe may have heard my prayers,
Perhaps the moon took pity on me,
Or maybe the deities liked what I offered.
My eyes
Your eyes
Weaved like an ancient clothe
Imbedded with seashells and bronze talismans
I was drawn deep into the black hole
Making me weak, overwhelmed, and hopeless
Your silhouette is still carved in me
Not like tattoo, but like a marble sculpture—
Soft, careful, delicate, and timeless masterpiece.
I called your name, I called you again
I shouted your name, I shouted it again
But all I heard was the echoes of my desperate voice

You were d
        r
          i
            f
              t
                i
                  n
                    g

slowly and slowly

like how the tides in the ocean started to rise

like a flat stone thrown into the surface of a lake—

carefully waiting it to bounce three times.

The last grain left—

Of my heart started to ache and

Crack, little by little

Grain turning to dust

Little by little

Dust by dust

Each of my being still breaks

Every time I see you…

Incense

They asked me to pray,
They asked me to beg the divinities,
They asked me to light a candle,
Or burn three incense every night.

I did it all
And each night I hope
That the divinities hear my prayers
That the candle may give me warmth and light
That the smoke of the incense may take my pleas,
Cries, and wishes—
To the universe and to anyone who may listen…

City Lights

I went to cities and to places I have never been
Where houses are like grains of rice
Put together side by side.
The loud noise,
The busy streets,
The sticky air,
The sweating palm of your hand as you consume
Your day wandering places
The sweat of a stranger
Pressing against your own skin
Colliding like falling stars in the night sky,
Drops of sweat mixed with your own
And the sudden longing of warmth and passion
I felt—
The urge to feel someone who can tame the raging snowstorm in me
Like a warm cup of coffee in the morning—simple and comforting
At night, some people go for rest

Some stay up and continue wandering, looking for their life

In unfamiliar corners and in foreign places, and—

I am here sitting, looking on the stars and the city lights—

City lights are stars on earth, they are solemn but tired

Beautiful but empty

Silent and chaotic

Something

I have always possessed a memory of a goldfish. I always forgot things, my eyeglasses, my laptop, my phone, and even my precious books. On the bright side, my mother has those magical powers of finding something and everything. Now, as I grow old, I still loses something but something I don't know. Something I can't name. But I feel something is missing in me—something which my mother can't find for me. Something that only, I can figure out myself.

You

I want silent days, rainy days, sunny days, and every day with you. A breakfast with you and to end my day within the warmth of your embrace. I want you to tell me that everything is going to be alright, even though the chaos found itself again in my mind. I want you to calm the storm in me. I want you and you only.

Help Is Available, Speak With Someone Today

I tried again
To kill myself
I tried to cut my wrist
And to drink some pills
Or to hang myself
I tried to look
For something pain—
less, something fast
and something not messy
isn't ironic?
I want to end my life
but afraid to feel
some pain?
maybe not,
maybe because
I felt too much
pain already

and I don't want
to feel pain again.
I tried to
kill myself again
Kill? I'm already dead!
I'm dead but I
tried to live—
leave everything,
so maybe this night
I'll try to kill myself,
again…

A Journey Is A Work Of Art

A journey is a work of art. It is like writing a poem. Word by word, you thought of the best figure of speech to contain the feeling and to express the longing. You can write it with rhyme—with the butter-smooth flow of words that roll on your tongue. You can write it in free verse, unnatural, unbounded, yet consistent, and meaningful. Or you can just write nothing. Stare at the blank page or the white screen of your laptop while watching your cursor. A journey, just like any work of art, is a process. A mixture of life's bittersweet scenarios. And the ability to turn your pain into a beautiful masterpiece.

This Town

The familiar walls of my empty room
The four corners that contain my prayers
Prayers for saving and prayers to end—
this miserable living.
I want to leave this town
This house
This room
and this life.
But how can I leave a thing that already
became a part of me?
Like my shadow in the rise of sun
The dream of escaping it when the sun sets
and the frustration to see it again in the morning.
I moved to places but this town
this town is in me.
Bad memories and happy memories mixed together
like how the ocean waves settles and kiss the sands
of shore.

I Am Writing This Poem Inside A Bus

The creaking sound of engine,

People sleeping,

Confused eyes typing,

The bumpy road,

and the smell of enclosed airconditioned room—

everything reminds me of the place I left.

The place where the morning breeze,

The rising sun,

and the foggy weather

screams a silent peace and tons of emptiness.

The swirling tornado-like sensation

of believing to start a new life in a new place,

the awkwardness of meeting a stranger's eyes,

and the unknown 'what if' of finding comfort,

warmth, and belongingness into someone's

embrace.

I am writing this poem inside a bus
going back to the place I once called—
home.

To Hurt Someone

To hurt someone is like throwing a stone on a lake, sea, or river. You can see how the stone bounces through the surface but left clueless on how deep it gets.

It's The Warmth That A Pair Of Socks Give

The coffee cup that settles empty on the table,

The creaking sounds of burning wood in the fireplace,

The dry and cold breeze of the wind—Everything

reminds me of you. The warmth of a pair of socks,

The comfort of my old cardigan, weaved through my flesh and

every fiber of my being—in every yarn of memories, laughter, and everything we shared.

Everything reminds me of you—on how a pair of coffee cups

clang in the morning, seeing you with my cardigan, preparing something.

On how our bodies merged while sitting in front of the fireplace,

Wanting some heat, 'cos everything seems to turn ice

And how the dry and cold breeze of the wind, still carries your scent

your name, and your voice…

The City I Don't Like…

I want to go to the city that I don't like. I want to laugh in the crowd of strangers around me. I want to cry when I hear a sad song in the dark room. I want to get wet in the rain for no reason. I want to smoke on unfamiliar streets and drink in new places. Where no one will ask—what happened? Why? How? There will be no worries, no tensions, no expectations. It is impossible for me to sit quietly in a corner of the room and pretend that my mind is in peace—when in reality a series of chaos commences in my brain. Has no one even noticed that I am not the same as before, something has changed in me. Something was lost, and gained, and still being searched for.

Part Of Me

So much of you lives within me,
from dusk till dawn,
smell of your celestial perfume,
your one and only maroon hat,
and your sunny-forced smiles.
all lives within me.
every love song, every poem,
each carry your name a piece of our love, my love
my eyes are reflection of your heart,
my smile, reflection of your soul
so much of you lives within me; too much.
and all that I had left are these,
all that's left are fragments of once hope of us.
yet the smell of your celestial perfume,
the color of your one and only maroon hat,
your sunny-forced smiles,
and every song and every poem
still echoes your name…

Emptiness

e

                                        m

p
t

                    i

n

e

                           s

s

To Whom It May Concern

I don't like date, grand gestures, and celebrations. I don't fancy roses, gifts, and cakes—except if it's blueberry cheesecake. But I like coffee, poetry, literature, small talks, musicals, jazz, and movies—little women is my go-to one. I am typical, complex, unpredictable, mentally unstable, gay boy.

Sometimes I like loud conversations and gatherings. But mostly, I prefer staying in my room, listening to my on-loop Spotify playlist, and staring blankly into my white-cracked ceiling. I smoke and occasionally drink. I am devastated, flawed, abandoned, lonely, and totally broken into pieces—like shards of glass.

I do write, play the violin and kalimba, and… I long for something—for someone. Which no words, rhymes, chords, stories, and movies could suffice. I long to be loved and cared by someone who sees me more than just my wounds and bruises. I need someone whom I can drink coffee with, have small talks, read poetry, or just someone who'll be there for me.

I already found that someone, but I am afraid to hint something. To make them know how much I admire their smile, posture, music, words, wit, heart, and soul.

You're the one who makes me believe in the goodness of this world, that even life is a mess—you're there to make things better.

So, if you're reading this or maybe not. I just want you to know that I always and will always admire you wholly—from afar.

Solitude

S

o   l   i   t   u   d   e

.

As I Walk Along The Streets Of Diliman

As the sun kissed me goodbye, I decided to take a walk along the streets of Diliman. People are exercising, some are having a small picnic with their family, others are sitting on those old-bricked benches, and college students are jogging—perhaps for their Physical Education requirement. I sauntered as I stared blankly at the orange sky where the trees seemed to be shy with one another—crown shyness, as they call it. As I heard the whisper of your name along with the cool breeze of the suburban atmosphere. I felt your skin pass through my bare hands like how the grains of sand fall on an hourglass. I thought about you and am with you—just in my mind. You were always there—out of my reach and out of my league.

Time To Grieve

If only I had given myself time to grieve and mourn the things I have lost, I would not be living death every day.

How Can I?

If the time comes that I will be meeting my old self, how can I say to them that ~~I failed to live their life?~~

I know that I will burn everything

The bamboo bridge we made to meet each other,

Our eyes that catch sparks but too scared to ignite,

Our skin that attracts like magnets,

and our heart that beats for each other.

I know that I will burn everything

Everything we build and dreamed of building—

will turn to ashes of sorrow *where silence may find its peace.*

~~I know that I will burn everything~~ —even you

S   o   r   u   n   ,

hide,

l e a v e,

Before you catch the fire—that will
EVENTUALLY BURN ME.

Never will I

How can I forgive myself? For not being the person I dreamed of.

Happiness Is A Choice?

They say that happiness is a choice, but for me, happiness comes with white, dull, bitter, and expensive pills.

About the Author

Benj Gabun Sumabat

Benj Gabun Sumabat is a second-year creative writing student from the University of the Philippines-Diliman, College of Arts and Letters. He currently lives in Diliman Quezon City but grew up in Ifugao and Cagayan Valley. He is an activist, poet, and writer. He mainly writes fiction, non-fiction, poetry, and short stories. His works have been published in some online literary journals, newspapers, and have also been featured in online art exhibits.

www.ingramcontent.com/pod-product-compliance
Lightning Source LLC
LaVergne TN
LVHW041552070526
838199LV00046B/1919